CENTER STAGE

WITHDRAWN

D0974602

CENTER STAGE

Adapted by Sarah Nathan

Based on the series created by Chris Thompson

Part One is based on the episode, "Start It Up," written by Chris Thompson

Part Two is based on the episode, "Hook It Up," written by Chris Thompson

DISNEP PRESS

NEW YORK

DANCE It UP

First Edition
1 3 5 7 9 10 8 6 4 2
J689-1817-1-12167

ISBN 978-1-4231-6335-0

For more Disney Press fun, visit www.disneybooks.com
Visit DisneyChannel.com

PART ONE

CHAPTER 1

EARLY ONE MORNING on a crowded outdoor train platform in Chicago, commuters were waiting for their train. Some were reading newspapers or drinking coffee as they stood around.

"Good morning!" Rocky Blue shouted, full of energy as she skipped onto the center of the platform. With her electric blue leggings and pink sweater, she brightened up the dull gray city landscape. Her long, dark hair hung loosely down past her shoulders as she smiled at the crowd.

"Ladies and gentlemen," CeCe Jones, Rocky's best friend, greeted everyone. She was dressed urban style, in chic cropped denim shorts over red tights and red knee-high socks. She tossed her long, layered red hair to the side.

"We're here for your commuting entertainment," Rocky continued as she worked the crowd. She was holding an MP3 player in a dock, ready to press PLAY.

CeCe passed a hat around. "If you like us, please give us a dollar," she pleaded. She handed the hat to one of the men in the crowd. "If you don't like us . . . Oh, who am I kidding?" she joked, laughing. "You're going to love us!" She thrust the hat into another man's hand. "Okay, pass it on, please." She looked over at her friend and grinned. "Hit it, Rocky."

Once the music started, the two best friends began to rock out their dance routine. People couldn't help but tap their feet and move to the beat. Soon everyone was grooving to the music and enjoying the show. Rocky and CeCe even pulled a few people into the center with them and taught them a couple of funky dance moves. Suddenly, the mundane morning wait for a train had turned into a real rocking party!

When the song ended, the girls smiled at each other and held their poses. CeCe reached for the tip hat that had been passed around and gave it to Rocky. She was eager to find out how much money they had made in tips.

"How'd we do? How'd we do?" CeCe asked, jumping up and down.

Rocky turned the hat upside down. "It's a stinkin' dime," she muttered.

CeCe turned to the commuters on the platform. "Oh, come on, people!" she cried. "Yesterday there was a guy here with a psychic cat named Mittens, and even *I* gave him a dollar!"

"Let's try this again," Rocky said, trying to appeal to the crowd. She smiled and pointed to herself. "I'm Rocky, and Red over there is CeCe."

CeCe smiled at the group around her. "And we're the only ones in our class who don't have cell phones," she added. The friends were hoping to make enough money to finally buy them!

"Plus, we need operations," CeCe chimed in. After seeing Rocky's stern look, she shrugged. "What?" she asked innocently. She was just trying to get some sympathy–or at least a quarter!

The hat traveled from hand to hand again. Rocky waited for it to get around the circle of people and back to her.

"How did we do this time?" CeCe asked when the hat came back to Rocky.

"Someone stole our dime," Rocky replied incredulously, turning the hat upside down again.

So much for the plan to make money with a train platform dance routine. At this rate, they'd never get cell phones!

♪ ♪ ♪

The next morning the television was blaring the show *Shake It Up, Chicago* as CeCe was getting ready for school. The TV show showcased the latest songs and the hottest dancers in Chicago. CeCe opened the window and yelled to the apartment upstairs. "Yo, Rocky, hustle it up! School starts in twenty!" How lucky was CeCe that her best friend lived in the same building!

At that moment, CeCe's mom came into the room. She was already dressed in her police uniform, ready to head to work. She flipped off the television set and then raised a window a few feet away. "Quit yelling!" she shouted out the window to her daughter. "You're going to wake the whole neighborhood!"

"Shhh!" CeCe scolded as she shut the window.

"Did you shush me?" her mom asked, walking over to CeCe.

CeCe faced her mom, blushing. "Well, I wouldn't have to yell if only . . ."

"I had a cell phone," her mother said, finishing her daughter's sentence.

"How'd you know I was going to say that?" CeCe asked.

"Sweetheart," her mother replied, smiling at her. "Those were your first words." She reached out and gave CeCe's shoulder a squeeze. "All right, I'm off to fight crime."

"Mom, you're a cop, not a superhero," CeCe said, her hands on her hips.

"A single mom raising two kids on her own *is* a superhero," she said. "The only reason I'm not wearing a cape is because I'm behind on the laundry." She threw her bag over her shoulder, chuckled to herself, and then headed for the door.

Just then, CeCe's younger brother, Flynn, came running into the room. "Bye, Mom!" he cried.

"Bye, Flynn," she said, reaching down and giving her son a big hug. She looked up at CeCe. "Don't forget to give your brother breakfast." Then she smiled and called, "Hey, love you." She blew them a kiss.

"Love you, too," the kids called back.

Flynn sat down at the breakfast table. He looked up at his big sister. "Can I get Toasted Tarts?"

CeCe shook her head disapprovingly. "Flynn, they're ninety percent sugar."

"Oh, do you have anything a hundred percent?" he asked, raising his eyebrows hopefully.

Just as CeCe was going to answer him, Rocky appeared on the fire escape. She climbed in through the window. "We've got five minutes to get to the train," she announced as she hopped inside the apartment.

"You live one flight up. How are you always late?" CeCe asked.

"Give me a break!" Rocky exclaimed. "That scary one-eyed pigeon was on the fire escape again!" She did her best to imitate the crazy one-eyed bird. "Let's go."

CeCe gestured to her little brother sitting at the table. "I can't. I have to get some food into Flynn."

A smile spread across Rocky's face. "One-minute breakfast?" she suggested. She crossed her arms over her chest.

Knowing what was coming, Flynn looked horrified. "Oh, no! Not one-minute breakfast!" he shouted. He took off toward his room.

"Get him!" the girls cried. They both lunged for him and brought him back to the table.

"In five, four, three, two . . . breakfast!" Rocky

and CeCe shouted as they sat Flynn down in a kitchen chair.

"You hate me, don't you?" Flynn asked, staring up at his sister.

"Can you eat a bowl of cereal in thirty seconds?" CeCe challenged.

He shook his head. "No. I only like it when it gets mushy with milk."

That gave CeCe an idea. "Okay, Rocky, hit it," she said.

Rocky poured cereal and milk into the blender and whirled the mixture together in a colorful mush.

Flynn put his head in his hands. "I want bacon!" he whined.

"We don't have any bacon," CeCe reminded him.

"And *why* is there no bacon?" he asked. "I bust my butt in third grade and all I ask for is a lousy strip of bacon." He peered over at the blended cereal and milk. "Eww."

"Okay. Here, take it to go," Rocky said, pouring the mixture into a plastic bag. She handed the bag to Flynn. "You know, breakfast is the most important meal of the day."

Flynn examined the contents of the bag. "It looks like a big bag of vomit."

"Yes, but it's the most *important* bag of vomit of the day," CeCe said.

She smiled at her little brother, and they all headed out the door to school. Who said she couldn't prepare a fast—and delicious—breakfast for Flynn?

CHAPTER 2

CECE AND ROCKY stood at their lockers just as the first bell of the school day was about to ring. CeCe got her books from inside her locker as Rocky scanned the hallway.

"Hottie alert! Hottie alert!" Rocky cried as she spied a good-looking guy walking by. "Could he be any cuter?" She sighed as he rushed by. He turned and smiled at Rocky before he continued to walk down the hallway.

"Hey, um, call me!" Rocky exclaimed, motioning with her hand on a nonexistent cell phone. "If I ever *get* a cell phone," she added sadly as he walked away.

"Hey, CeCe, Rocky, wassup?" said Deuce Martinez, one of their friends. He swaggered over to them with his earphones hanging around his neck.

"Hey, Deuce," the girls replied, smiling at their good friend.

"Check it out, chicas," Deuce said, with a sly grin on his face. He opened his hand, which held his latest prized possession. Deuce was forever trying to sell them something. He winked at his friends. "Two tickets for Lady Gaga, fifty bucks, obstructed view."

Rocky raised her eyebrows. "*How* obstructed?" she asked curiously.

"Ladies room, stall three," Deuce admitted, turning red with embarrassment.

CeCe shook her head emphatically. "As tempting as that is," she explained, "we're saving for cell phones."

"Are you sure?" Deuce asked. He flashed them his charming smile. "I'll throw in a complimentary watch," he said, pulling up his sleeve.

Rocky laughed. "You sold us *these* watches," she said, pointing to the watch already on her wrist. "Mine has the big hand and hers has the little one." She pointed to CeCe, who nodded in agreement.

"I begged you to buy the warranty," Deuce told her. Before the girls walked away, he reached into his bag. "Not so fast, I got something that's *perfect* for you ladies. Check this out." He handed CeCe a flyer.

"*Shake It Up, Chicago*. Auditions on the tenth, looking for teen background dancers thirteen and up,'" CeCe read. She looked up at Deuce. "Get out of here! *Shake It Up, Chicago*? It's only like, our favorite TV dance show in the world!" She bounced up and down with excitement.

"Those dancers are sick," Rocky commented to Deuce.

With a longing stare, CeCe sighed. "Oh, I would *so* kill you to be on that show."

"Oh, I would so *let* you," Rocky replied.

Deuce checked his watch. There were definitely fewer people in the hallway now. "Hey, what time you got?" he asked.

CeCe looked at her watch. "Eight," she replied casually.

"Thirteen," Rocky added, noticing the little hand on her watch.

Taking off down the hallway, Deuce called over his shoulder, "Late for English!"

CeCe and Rocky shrugged. Good thing that they were always together so that telling time was possible!

The girls suddenly spotted someone walking

toward them. "Hello, peoples. I am Gunther," a tall blond boy announced.

"And *I* am Tinka," a blond girl who looked just like him added.

"And we are . . ." Gunther continued, giving Rocky and CeCe a snide look.

"The Hessenheffers!" the duo said in unison. They were both dressed in black sequined jackets over loud, bright outfits. They struck a pose as if they were onstage.

CeCe rolled her eyes. "We know who you are," she said, not impressed. They all did go to the same school, after all!

Tinka eyed the flyer in CeCe's hand. "I see you have a flyer for the *Shake It Up, Chicago* local popular television dance program," she said in her heavy accent.

"We also have a flyer," Gunther told them. He displayed the piece of paper proudly. "Now is your chance to exit from the audition gracefully, hanging your heads like dogs. Woof, woof," he and Tinka barked.

"Wait a second, *Stinka*," CeCe said. She couldn't believe how rude they were being. Well, two could play that game!

"Oh! That was a good one!" Rocky exclaimed, realizing CeCe's new nickname for Tinka. She crossed her arms and glared at the brother and sister.

CeCe took a moment to gloat. "Was that not a good one? That was so good!" Then she remembered that the Hessenheffers were still standing in front of her. She turned back to them. "Why *wouldn't* we audition?" she asked them. "We are the *best* dancers in Chicago." CeCe put a hand on her hip and tossed her hair to the side.

"Don't be loony," Gunther told her. "You're not even the best dancers in this *hallway*," he said, rolling his eyes.

Just then, the bell for first period rang. Tinka

put her hand to her ear. "Is that the bell for class? Or is it one of your cell phones that don't exist?" She and her brother pulled out their cell phones and laughed. "Text us!" they exclaimed, smirking.

CeCe glared at the Hessenheffers. Did everyone know that they were cell phone-less? "Come on, Rocky," she said. She didn't want to be late for class.

But no matter what CeCe's watch said, this was going to be a *long* day. How was she going to concentrate when all she could think about were the *Shake It Up, Chicago* auditions?

CHAPTER 3

AND INDEED, it *was* a long day. Rocky and CeCe couldn't wait for the end of the school day. As they walked home from school, CeCe suddenly came up with a great idea. Once they were outside their apartment building, CeCe turned to her best friend.

"Hey, we should practice some moves for the audition," she suggested. Ever since Deuce had handed her that flyer, all she could think about was being a dancer on *Shake It Up, Chicago*.

"Yeah, about that," Rocky said seriously. Her voice was full of concern. "I don't think I'm ready for this. Maybe Gunther and Tinka are right."

"Why would you listen to anything they say?" CeCe asked. "What are you, *loony*?" She twirled her finger around her ear just like Gunther had done. She even vamped his strong accent.

"Maybe I am, but I'm still not going. It's too scary," Rocky said. She slipped her backpack off her shoulders and sat down on the front steps of their apartment building.

CeCe moved closer to her friend. "Oh, come on, Rock, don't do this again," she pleaded.

"Do what?" Rocky replied innocently.

"Be *you*!" CeCe cried. "Talk yourself out of doing something before it even happens." She sat down on the step next to her friend. "All our lives we've dreamed about being professional dancers. Now we can see if we're good enough."

Rocky leaned in closer. "I think there's going to be big kids there," she said nervously.

Just then, Rocky's older brother, Ty, came out of the front door and bounced down the steps. CeCe was relieved to see him. Maybe he could talk some sense into his little sister. She called him over.

"Ty, could you please talk to your sister?" she asked. "She's too scared to audition for *Shake It Up, Chicago*."

Ty laughed. "That's because she can't do *this*," he said. He showed off one of his signature dance moves.

"Uh-huh!" Rocky replied, taking the dare. "I can do that." She jumped up and mimicked his move. She even added some of her own flair.

Ty raised his eyebrows. "All right, but you can't do *this*." He stepped up his game and strutted across the sidewalk in a backwards moonwalk.

"Oh, yeah!" Rocky replied, again showing off her dancing ability. "In my sleep."

Her older brother smiled at her. "Good," he said. "Do that at the audition tomorrow and you've got nothing to worry about."

"Ty, you're really good. You should audition with us," CeCe commented.

"No thanks. I don't dance for 'The Man,'" he told her. He puffed his chest out proudly. He watched a pretty girl stroll past and began to shuffle his feet. "But I *do* dance for the *wo*-man." He pointed to the girl and shot her a cool smile. "Hey! Wassup baby!" he called out and started to chase after her.

CeCe turned to Rocky with a knowing look. As sure as Ty was about winning over that girl, CeCe was sure that Rocky would be going to the audition for *Shake It Up, Chicago*. Their dream of dancing on TV was about to come true!

♪ ♪ ♪

CeCe and Rocky looked up at the large metal doors of the downtown theater where *Shake It Up, Chicago* was filmed. They went in and were blown away by all the amazing dancers in the room. There was a full-on dance party going on!

"Wow!" CeCe gasped as she took in the scene. The brightly lit stage was crowded with kids doing all kinds of awesome dance moves.

Rocky saw a group of teenagers dancing and clutched her bag. "Big kids! Big kids!" she cried anxiously. "I *told* you there would be big kids."

CeCe ignored Rocky's nervousness. She was focused on the guy across the room. "Look, there's Gary Wilde, the host of *Shake It Up, Chicago*." She paused for a second as she watched him. He was dressed in a green shirt under a black vest, and his brown hair was perfectly styled. As the camera rolled, he stepped up on a platform. "He looks taller on TV," CeCe whispered, noting that without the platform he was actually quite short.

Rocky took a quick glance at the host. "Really? Here's an idea, let's go home and check!" she exclaimed as she dashed for the large double doors that led out of the studio.

"*No! Rocky!* You're going to do it!" CeCe told her. She grabbed her friend's arm firmly and pulled her back.

Rocky struggled a little and unfortunately bumped into one of the dancers on the set. He was spinning on his back.

CeCe looked over and quickly apologized. "Oh! Sorry, upside-down guy. My bad."

Rocky surveyed the dance floor. Everyone was doing really sophisticated moves! More dancers were spinning on their backs, and some were dancing on their knees. "CeCe? Does anyone here dance on their feet?" she asked with her mouth gaping open.

Gary Wilde did a little backward glide as he slid away from the conversation with the director. "Hope you brought your hoodie because when Gary Wilde hits the floor, it gets a little cooler," Gary said with a coy wink. Then he spotted Rocky and CeCe. "You two remind me of little tiny fairies that live in the woods," he said.

CeCe perked up, even though that was a pretty odd comment! "Do you need fairies?" she asked, eagerly pointing back and forth between herself and Rocky. "'Cause we can be fairies."

"Do you want me to autograph your picture of me?" Gary asked as if he were on autopilot. His fans were always asking him for autographs, and he was always ready for them.

"Oh, we don't have a picture of you," Rocky gushed nervously. She couldn't believe that she was talking to the host of Shake It Up, Chicago!

Gary flashed the girls his TV-star grin. "That's all right, I have some. Lucky girls," he said as he fanned a few large, glossy head shots of himself. He handed them over to Rocky. Then he got distracted and walked away.

CeCe turned to Rocky. "Well, are you ready to do this?"

"No," Rocky said, shaking her head. She couldn't believe how calm CeCe seemed! Didn't she see all these amazing dancers around them? "Aren't you the least bit nervous?" she asked.

"I don't get nervous," CeCe said superconfidently.

Rocky took a deep breath. She tried to be as confident as CeCe.

The music got louder, and Rocky and CeCe joined the dancers on the dance floor in the center of the studio. The floor changed colors as the strobe lights flared and the beat grew more intense. The friends caught on to the routine quickly. Together they rocked out the steps as the spotlights shone on the dancers.

Gary was standing on the side of the stage watching the contestants. He held a clipboard and made notes. When the song was over, Gary strolled onto the dance floor. "Great job," he said to the kids. "You're all moving on to the next round!"

Everyone on the dance floor squealed with excitement.

"Except for you, you, you, and you," Gary said, pointing to a few unlucky people.

Rocky and CeCe let out a huge sigh of relief. They were through to the next round! Off on the side of the stage, Rocky and CeCe huddled together, shocked that they had made the first cut.

"I can't believe we made it this far!" CeCe exclaimed.

Gunther and Tinka came up beside them. "Neither can we," Gunther said in disbelief, mimicking CeCe's and Rocky's squeal.

"All right, kids," Gary said to the group, still holding his clipboard. "I only have six openings for background dancers. So, one last step. It's the spotlight dance!" He paused and walked around the contestants. "It's just you, your moves, and ten thousand kilowatts of hot, white light highlighting your every flaw. And remember, have fun!" He stepped off the dance floor and stood by the cameras.

A guy strutted up to the center of the stage and spun, popped, and flipped like a pro. CeCe and Rocky watched in awe. When he got off the stage, Gary was standing there. "All right! You're good, but you just don't have the look we want," he said, slapping the kid on the back. "Next!"

"That guy was great and they let him go?" Rocky asked in complete shock. "What chance do *we* have?"

CeCe checked out all the people still standing around waiting for their final auditions. "A better chance now that he's gone," she said realistically.

"Next up, Rocky Blue!" Gary called out.

CeCe gave Rocky a hug. "That's you. Good luck!"

Rocky tightened her grip around CeCe's body. She wouldn't let go!

Laughing uncomfortably, CeCe was desperately trying to pull away from Rocky's hug. Everyone was looking at them. "Rock, Rocky, let go. Rocky. Let. Go!" CeCe urged her friend. She struggled and was finally able to free her arm. Rocky slipped down and latched onto CeCe's knees like a scared toddler on the first day of nursery school. Finally, CeCe pushed Rocky out onto the dance floor. She spun on her knees and wound up in the middle of the stage.

"There you are," Gary said when Rocky arrived on the dance floor.

Rocky slowly stood up. She was a little dazed and felt really, really nervous!

"Let's see what you got," the host said. He looked up at the sound booth. "Hit it," he directed the DJ and then took his post on the side of the stage to watch.

The music cued up, and Rocky started to sway to the pulsing beat. She twirled and popped and forgot all about the people staring at her as she danced.

CeCe sighed with relief. She watched as her friend gave way to the music. Rocky was amazing! When the music ended, Rocky beamed and enjoyed the applause. She had nailed her audition!

Gary stopped Rocky before she could leave the stage. "I'm sorry," he said in a solemn tone. Then a smile broke out across his face. "But, I'm afraid you're *in*!"

"Seriously? I'm *in*?" Rocky screamed, jumping up and down. "I'm going to be on the show every week?" She reached over and slapped Gary on the back as if they'd been friends for years.

"Thanks, *Gare*," she said with ease. She raced over to CeCe, giddy with excitement. "I called him 'Gare'," she whispered.

"All right, next dancer," Gary announced. "CeCe Jones."

Rocky grabbed CeCe's hand. "Remember, don't get nervous," she told her. She looked over her shoulder at the lit-up dance floor. She now had the confidence of a superstar. "It's not as scary as it looks."

"Nervous?" CeCe scoffed. "I've been waiting for this my whole life." She sauntered out to the bright dance floor. She straightened her army jacket and adjusted her sparkling T-shirt. She was so ready to show *Shake It Up, Chicago* what she had!

Gary took one look at CeCe and grinned. "Ah! Young, funky, great look . . . You're perfect," he told her. He leaned in closer to whisper in her ear. "Now if you can just dance without falling on your butt, you're in." He turned on his designer-shoe heel and headed offstage.

CeCe laughed nervously. The room went dark, and a single spotlight shone down on her. She couldn't breathe. She couldn't move. She was frozen!

"CeCe," Rocky called from the side of the stage. She waved her hand to get CeCe's attention. She didn't know what CeCe was doing, but it sure wasn't dancing! Rocky knew that CeCe had to start to move now that the music had started. This was her turn to shine! If she didn't dance, she couldn't get picked to be on the show. "You have to dance!" she called out.

Paralyzed in the bright light, CeCe just stared straight ahead. "Can't dance, might fall on butt," she said as if she were a robot low on batteries.

"But Gary said you were perfect," Rocky told her as she moved closer to her. She put her hands on CeCe's shoulders. She had to get her friend to focus! She had to get her to dance!

"Yeah, no pressure there," CeCe said sarcastically, still unable to move.

Offstage, Gary shook his head and looked at his watch. "Tick-tock," he said. "Is she going to dance or not?"

Rocky tried to loosen up CeCe. She moved CeCe's arms the way a puppeteer would. "Oh, she's going to dance!" Rocky cried. But Rocky's attempt to get CeCe moving was a complete disaster.

"Sorry, kid," Gary said to CeCe as he walked onstage. The song was over, and so was CeCe's chance at getting on the show.

"But, but, Gary!" Rocky pleaded. "She's got the look!"

Gary shook his head. If CeCe didn't dance, she couldn't be on the show. CeCe was devastated. She tore through the double doors and out of the studio.

"CeCe, wait!" Rocky shouted. She chased after her friend. She couldn't believe that CeCe had frozen onstage and then bolted. That was something she was scared *she* was going to do! Rocky would give anything to rewind the scene and play it again differently. How was she going to be a dancer on *Shake It Up, Chicago* without her best friend?

CHAPTER 4

ROCKY RACED UP the steps to the train platform. CeCe had left the studio so quickly that she hadn't even taken her bag. Rocky lugged both her bag and CeCe's to the outside waiting area. She sighed when she spotted her best friend sitting on a bench at the far end of the platform. CeCe was slumped over with her head in her hands. She looked really upset.

"You all right?" Rocky asked as she hurried over to her.

CeCe sniffed and looked at her friend. "No, Rocky, I'm *not* all right," she said, lifting up her head. She took a deep breath, reliving the horrible stage-fright moment. "I froze up there. This was the most embarrassing day of my life." She sighed and then continued, "I walk around thinking I'm so cool, but in real life, I'm a loser." She looked at her best friend sadly.

"That's ridiculous!" Rocky exclaimed. "I can't remember one time where you *ever* acted like a loser."

"Really?" CeCe asked. She gave her friend a quizzical look. "Remember when we were at camp and I wanted to race those canoes?" She winced at the memory.

"They were very unstable," Rocky said, coming to her defense. "CeCe Jones is *not* a loser. CeCe Jones is a girl who has the guts to try all these crazy things, and I, as her BFF, get to try them, too." She smiled and hoped her friend would listen to her. She didn't like seeing CeCe so distraught.

CeCe cocked her head to the side. She took a moment to consider Rocky's statement. "That's true," she admitted slowly. "In many ways, I'm awesome." She laughed and grinned at her best friend.

"You *are* awesome," Rocky confirmed. "And, uh, I'm kind of awesome, too," she added, smiling widely.

"No, no, no, you're awesome-*er*," CeCe corrected her. She reached out and hugged her friend.

Just then, Gunther and Tinka walked over to where Rocky and CeCe were sitting. "Say hello to the newest background dancers of *Shake It Up, Chicago*," Gunther declared. "I am Gunther, *und* this is . . ." He whipped out a flashlight and shone it on his sister. Tinka struck a pose and held an exaggerated look of surprise. "Oh, no! Tinka has frozen in her spotlight!" He and Tinka burst out laughing at the re-enactment of CeCe's audition.

Rocky and CeCe were not laughing. They watched as Gunther and Tinka walked off, giddy with excitement that they had been chosen to dance on the show. Rocky looked back at her best friend. She was already rolling her eyes at the Hessenheffers. She knew CeCe would be okay. They would get through this tough time together!

♪ ♪ ♪

A few days later, on Saturday morning, Rocky headed downstairs to CeCe's apartment. She slipped through the window, still dressed in her pajamas and her pink-and-white striped robe.

"Hey, hey, hey," Rocky said, making a beeline

for the refrigerator and grabbing a carton of milk. She poured herself a glass.

"What are you still doing in your pj's?" CeCe asked, looking at her friend in shock. "I was just about to pick you up and take you to the show!"

Rocky plopped down in a chair at the kitchen table. "Now I don't want to be on *Shake It Up, Chicago,*" Rocky said. She took a large sip of milk. "I mean, it's going to be no fun without you!" She tried to force a smile.

"Gunther and Tinka will be there," CeCe replied, trying to sound comforting.

"Now I don't even want to *watch* the show," Rocky told her, slumped at the table.

CeCe stood next to Rocky. "I may not be on *Shake It Up, Chicago,* but I'm still going to be there to support you," she replied. "We're totally in this together."

Rocky shrugged. "It doesn't matter, it's too late," she told her. "I was supposed to be there at nine and it's eight-thirty. I look like a zombie, and I haven't even brushed my teeth!" She shook her head in defiance.

CeCe grinned. "We'll make it," she told her friend. "Open," she directed. Even though Rocky had just taken a large gulp of milk, CeCe shoved an electric toothbrush in her mouth. "We'll run up to your place and grab some clothes. That sound good?"

Rocky couldn't reply. She was spitting out minty milk everywhere! It appeared that CeCe wasn't going to take no for an answer!

"La, la, la, la," CeCe sang out as she brushed her friend's teeth. She held out a glass. "Spit."

Rocky did what she was told.

"Come on, come on, come on!" CeCe exclaimed as she rushed Rocky toward the door. "Later, Mom!" she called as they ran out.

After the two girls left, Flynn strolled into the kitchen and spotted the glass of milk on the table. Having no idea that the glass was full of spit-out milk, he raised the glass to take a sip. He was pretty thirsty.

"Mmm, minty!" he exclaimed as he swallowed. He didn't know what kind of fancy milk his sister had left on the table for him, but it sure was delicious. Now this was a breakfast that he could appreciate!

CHAPTER 5

WHEN CECE AND ROCKY arrived at the *Shake It Up, Chicago* set, the show was just about to begin. Bright, colorful lights lit up the stage and the dance floor. The dancers were facing the cameras. In the center of the action was Gary, waiting for his cue to start the show.

"Here's your host, Gary Wilde!" a voice suddenly boomed from the speakers above.

A cameraman waved at Gary, and he smiled

at the camera. He gripped his microphone and greeted the television audience. "Hello, Chicago!" he sang out.

The crowd of dancers all cheered. "You're watching the show that has it all. New music, new videos, and the dance music you'll be moving to at home tomorrow. This is . . ." He paused for the dramatic effect of having everyone wait. "*Shake It Up, Chicago!*" he finally said. He flashed his super-toothy grin. "I'm your host, Gary Wilde," he said. Then he leaned into the camera. "And I *am* this tall in real life." He ducked out of the shot, and the dancers filled the stage.

Rocky knew that it was now or never. She pulled on CeCe's arm. But her friend was not budging from her spot on the sidelines.

"Come with me," Rocky begged.

"I can't. I'm not on the show," CeCe said. She felt a little self-conscious—all the dancers who had been selected for the show were enthusiastically dancing onstage. She had botched up her audition and didn't deserve to be there.

"Yeah, well, I *am* on the show and like you said, we're in this together," Rocky told her. She pulled out a pair of handcuffs from her back pocket and slapped them on her wrist and then on CeCe's!

CeCe looked at her friend incredulously. "What are you doing?" she asked.

"Not letting you miss the dream," Rocky said firmly. She pulled her shocked friend up onstage. "Come on."

Now that they were standing on the stage with the bright lights and the music blaring, CeCe felt even more awkward. "No, I can't!" she insisted.

Rocky was not about to let her best friend give up hope. She pulled CeCe toward the stage. They both struggled to keep their balance. Then, Rocky started to dance. She knew that once CeCe felt the beat and began to move, she'd be fine. "Move it!" Rocky instructed.

Because they were joined at the wrists by the handcuffs, dancing was a little bit of a challenge for them. The two friends kept bumping into each other as well as other people on the dance floor!

"Ooh, ooh, sorry!" CeCe shouted as she ran into another dancer.

Rocky tried to smile as she struggled to dance with CeCe. She didn't want to cause a scene, but there was no way she was doing this show without her friend.

"Where'd you get the handcuffs?" CeCe asked as she tried to move to the left as Rocky moved to the right.

"They're your mom's," Rocky told her. "I'm sure she won't miss them for a day."

CeCe gulped. She wasn't so sure about that. A cop needed handcuffs for patrolling. In fact, at that very moment, CeCe's mom was dealing with a criminal. She was holding the guy's hands behind his back and reaching for her handcuffs.

"All right, dirtbag, hands behind your back!" she told him. She searched her pockets and came up empty-handed. She couldn't let the crook know that she didn't have handcuffs so she quickly improvised. "And keep them behind your back. Unless you want me to put these handcuffs on you," she said. She leaned in closer to him. "They're *really* super-pinchy."

The guy seemed to take her word for it and kept his hands behind his back.

CeCe and Rocky could attest to that pinchy fact! The more they struggled, the more their wrists hurt from the handcuffs. But they soon fell into the same groove and started to dance as they never had before. Their moves were perfectly in sync and they were getting lots of attention. Their enthusiasm for dancing was contagious!

The cameraman took note and zoomed in on the two girls.

At CeCe's apartment, Deuce, Ty, and Flynn were camped out on the couch watching the live show. While they expected to see Rocky onstage, they were shocked to see CeCe front and center!

Deuce sat up and leaned closer to the television set. "Whoa, what's CeCe doing on TV?" he asked.

"I don't know," Ty said, shaking his head. "For a girl who isn't on the show, she's on the show a *lot*."

As the boys stared at the television set, Flynn rolled his eyes in disgust. "Sure, she has time to dance on TV, but she can't pick up a lousy pack of bacon," he said, pouting. He still couldn't believe the cereal his sister had made for him the other day!

The song ended and the dancers on *Shake It Up, Chicago* all cheered. Gary leaped onto the stage and spoke into his microphone. "That's right, people, dancing *so* good, it should be illegal," he said, making reference to the handcuffs on Rocky and CeCe. He grinned and winked at the camera. "We'll be right back with more music, more dancing, and the premiere of Usher's newest video, right here on *Shake It Up, Chicago!*"

Gary held his pose until he heard the director's voice.

"And we're *out*," the man with the clipboard shouted. He held up two fingers to the crowd. "Two minutes, people!"

CeCe turned to Rocky. She was beaming. "We *totally* just danced on TV!"

"And we *totally* rocked it!" Rocky added happily. She knew her idea of getting CeCe to dance on the show was brilliant. They headed toward the side of the stage to take a break while the cameras were off.

"Girls!" Gary called as they rushed past him.

The girls looked at each other nervously. They were afraid this was coming! Suddenly, Rocky's idea didn't seem so great.

CeCe looked over at her friend. "And we're *totally* getting thrown out of here."

CHAPTER 6

THE BEST FRIENDS held their breath as they watched Gary stare at their handcuffed wrists.

"Well, well, well," he said. "That was *quite* a little show you ladies put on out there."

"Look, I'm sorry," CeCe blurted out. "But please don't fire Rocky. It's my fault."

"She's wrong," Rocky said. "*I'm* the one who chained us together because she belongs here."

She pointed to CeCe. "She's an awesome dancer."

"Wrong!" Gary challenged. He looked at both of them seriously. "You're *both* awesome dancers."

CeCe gasped. Did Gary Wilde just give them both a compliment? He liked how they danced? This was all too good to be true!

"You've got the skills, you've got the look," he continued. "But what you pulled out there was just weird and unexpected." He paused and narrowed his eyes at the girls.

CeCe took a deep breath. Were they about to get kicked out of the studio? Was Rocky going to get thrown off the show?

Gary started to smile. "And I *liked* it!" he exclaimed, surprising the girls. He pointed his finger at them. "But you pull something like that again and you are off the show." He moved past them, not saying another word.

The girls shared a look of disbelief. Did he just say what they thought he said? CeCe pulled

Rocky along as she followed the host. "Wait a second," she said when she was next to him. "To be off the show must mean I'm *on* the show?" she asked.

Gary turned and considered the two girls in front of him. He eyed their outfit choices and their overall appearance. "Yeah. You two got that whole 'it' factor," he told them with a smile.

"Thank you, Gary!" CeCe and Rocky screeched. "We won't let you down."

Just then, the assistant director walked by and made his announcement to the crowd. "And in five, four, three . . ." He signaled the cameraman, who started to film the dancers onstage. The show was back on the air!

CeCe lunged toward the dance floor with Rocky attached to her wrist. "Let's do this thing!" she cheered. Feeling the tug of Rocky's arm, she smiled at her friend. "Rocky, you can let us loose now," she said, laughing. There was no way that she was going to bolt for the doors. She was a dancer on *Shake It Up, Chicago!*

Rocky pulled their wrists up and studied the handcuffs closely. "Where's the secret button?" she asked, eyeing the lock.

"What secret button?" CeCe asked.

"You know, the secret button that opens the handcuffs," Rocky said. "Duh."

"It's called a key!" CeCe shouted. "Where's the key?"

Back at home, Flynn was still stretched out on the couch watching the show. When he saw Rocky and his sister struggling, he couldn't help but smirk. He pulled the handcuff key from his pocket and dangled it proudly. Ah, payback is sweet! he thought.

♪ ♪ ♪

"We got mail from *Shake It Up, Chicago!*" Rocky cheered as she came in through the window to CeCe's apartment. She waved the envelopes in front of CeCe, who yelled and grabbed one. The two girls ripped them open at the same time.

"Whoa!" CeCe exclaimed.

"Forty dollars *each!*" Rocky shouted. They had gotten their first paycheck from the show. "That's *every* week!" The impact of having an awesome new job was slowly sinking in. They were finally going to be able to buy cell phones!

"Whoa!" CeCe said again, unable to comprehend this new turn of events.

"Okay," Rocky said, thinking for a moment. "We have to take fifty dollars and buy your mom new handcuffs. Twenty dollars for the thrift-store dance clothes, and eight dollars for transportation." She drew equations with her finger, sketching out the numbers in the air. Her face formed into a frown when she realized what the total was. "That leaves us with two bucks."

"Whoa," CeCe repeated, her shoulders slumping. That wasn't such good news!

"But next week, we get to keep the whole eighty dollars," Rocky said brightly. The girls grinned at each other. They both knew what they were going to do with *that* paycheck. It was a no-brainer!

"Cell phones!" they cheered in unison as they danced around the kitchen.

Their celebration was cut short when Flynn suddenly stormed into the apartment. He was carrying a shopping bag from the grocery store. He sat down at the table and pulled out a package.

CeCe sighed and looked at her little brother. Couldn't her and Rocky have just a few more minutes to bask in the glory of their first paycheck?

Flynn looked at his sister and Rocky and pointed to the package on the table. "Bacon. Cook it," he ordered.

The girls looked at Flynn and laughed. Cooking bacon would be nothing compared to the drama of the past few days. Doing that was not going to ruin their good mood *or* their first paycheck dance. They were both officially dancers on *Shake It Up, Chicago*. And nothing was better than that!

PART TWO

After an awesome performance on the train platform,
CeCe and Rocky struck funky poses.

Rocky's brother, Ty, showed off one of his signature
dance moves.

Rocky nailed her *Shake It Up, Chicago* audition!

"CeCe Jones is a girl who has the guts to try all these crazy things, and, I, as your BFF, get to try them, too," Rocky said.

Gunther and Tinka, two of *Shake It Up, Chicago's* newest castmates, mocked CeCe for having stage fright.

Ty, along with Rocky and CeCe's friend Deuce, were shocked to see CeCe and Rocky dancing on TV!

CeCe and Rocky were perfectly in sync—even when they were handcuffed together!

Rocky showed CeCe an awesome new dance routine.

"Suckers!" CeCe's brother Flynn snickered as he sat down on the steps.

"I'm going to show you a move the ladies will love,"
Ty told Flynn.

Ty was shocked when he finally met Destiny.

Ty was not willing to give up the fight for Destiny's attention so easily.

Gary revved up the crowd as he introduced the *Shake It Up, Chicago* dancers.

In the middle of the dance, CeCe turned to Rocky.
"Ready?" she asked.

CeCe and Rocky rocked the dance floor to show Gary
what he would be missing if he fired them.

CHAPTER 1

CECE JONES AND ROCKY BLUE were hanging out on the stoop in front of their apartment building, watching people stroll by. Just then, a boy started pounding on a garbage can as if it were a drum. CeCe and Rocky smiled at each other and began to move to the beat. Dancing was their most favorite thing to do ever!

Rocky's brother Ty opened the door to bring out the trash and took out a shaker to add to the beat. Then he started to dance.

As the beat grew louder, the girls couldn't help but do even fancier dance routines. It was as if they were onstage. The drummer handed sticks to his friend passing by on a bike. The biker found another can to bang on and added his own beat to the music.

Rocky smiled as she danced. This is what she loved about living in the heart of Chicago. There was always some pickup band—with instruments or even just garbage cans! It really was an awesome place to live.

The beat got louder, and CeCe and Rocky got more into their impromptu dance party. How awesome was this!

At that moment, CeCe's little brother, Flynn, threw open the front door and raced outside. He looked around at the group and shook his head. "Hey, knock it off!" he scolded. "Some of us still like naps!"

Rocky gulped. She glanced over at CeCe, who ignored her little brother and counted out the beat for the song.

"Two, three, four!" CeCe shouted and the drumming continued.

Rocky started dancing again, not paying attention to Flynn's request for quiet.

"Well, it's only fair to tell you that five minutes ago I called the cops," Flynn announced proudly. Instantly, the group dispersed. CeCe, Rocky, Ty, and the two drummers ran down the street, far away from the apartment building's stoop. They didn't want to get in trouble!

"Suckers," Flynn snickered as he sat down on the steps. He was pleased with himself—his plan had worked and the street was peaceful once again. What did these people think? The whole city was the *Shake It Up, Chicago* dance set? He smiled happily, pleased to hear the sweet sounds of silence.

♪ ♪ ♪

On Monday morning, CeCe and Rocky headed to school. The weekend was still fresh in their minds. After all, they had just danced on the hit show *Shake It Up, Chicago* two days before. As they walked down the corridor to their lockers, CeCe turned to Rocky. "I wonder if anyone saw us on *Shake It Up, Chicago* Saturday," she asked, looking around.

As the girls turned the corner, there was a roar of applause. A smile spread across Rocky's face as she took in all the admiring fans that were smiling at them.

"I'd say they did," Rocky stated happily. "Is this all for us?" she asked. She headed over to her locker to grab her books.

"Make way, make way," their friend Deuce Martinez suddenly called out, pushing through the crowd to get to CeCe and Rocky. He was holding a video camera. "I need a two-shot of the stars."

Rocky looked at Deuce curiously. "What are you doing?" she asked.

"I'm making a documentary for my video class," he explained, holding up his camera. "No pressure," he told them. "But it's half my grade, and if you guys are lame, I'm looking at summer school."

The girls turned to their lockers and Deuce walked away, turning the camera on himself to document the beginning of the video. "Their climb to the lofty heights of stardom was meteoric," he stated with dramatic flair. "Imagine these two young losers—pathetic, shabby, unwashed nobodies one day and local superstars the next. How does it feel?" he wondered aloud.

CeCe and Rocky caught the end of Deuce's recording, and they *weren't* happy. Deuce pointed his camera at CeCe and Rocky as they headed toward him.

"How does *this* feel?" CeCe asked, poking him hard in the chest.

Deuce squealed and backed away. He might have to rethink his take on the story!

At that moment, everyone's attention went to the large screen hanging in the hallway. The morning announcements were about to begin, and the students gathered around anxiously to watch.

"Good morning, John Hughes High. This is Ty Blue with your pre-homeroom report." Ty gave his best TV anchor smile for the camera. He was wearing a spiffy black hat and a gray vest. "First up," he announced, "a special shout out to my own sister, Rocky Blue, who's now on *Shake It Up, Chicago* with her unbelievably talented BFF, CeCe Jones!"

Rocky pulled on CeCe's arm. "How much

did that cost you?" she whispered to her.

"Ten bucks, but it was worth it," she said, grinning. Ten dollars was a small price to pay for all the attention they were getting this morning!

Ty then began to announce the day's news. "I checked out lunch today," Ty told the attentive crowd. He leaned in closer to the camera. "And it seems to be fried sea horses again." Laughing, he winked at the audience. *"Bon appétit!"*

"Hey, you two," one of the cutest boys in school called out to CeCe and Rocky.

CeCe couldn't believe her eyes. *"Oi mamacita!"* she cried. She watched as he led a group of kids over to where they were standing. "It's the cool kids!" she exclaimed.

"And they're coming over here," Rocky added nervously.

"Hey, I'm Joshua," the cute guy said as he walked up to them. He was wearing a black jacket and a blue T-shirt. "Saw you on *Shake*

It Up, Chicago. You want to sit at our table at lunch today?"

CeCe swooned. "Yes!" she exclaimed.

"No!" Rocky shouted with authority.

"Yes," CeCe repeated.

"No," Rocky said again.

"Yes, yes!" CeCe shouted.

Rocky took a step forward. "No," she said firmly. She crossed her arms across her chest and turned to Joshua and his friends. "Before we were dancing on TV, the only time you guys looked at us was to copy off our homework," she told him.

Joshua put his hand on the locker above Rocky's head and leaned in closer to her. "What about tomorrow?" he asked, looking directly at her.

Rocky took one look into Joshua's dreamy eyes and smelled the clean scent of his hair. She couldn't believe how charming he was! "Oh, we're *definitely* free tomorrow," she said quickly, giggling nervously.

Joshua smiled and nodded to his friends to keep moving along down the hall.

Watching the group walk away, CeCe exhaled heavily. She threw her arm around Rocky's shoulders. "And so our rocket ship to superstardom takes off!" she announced. "First, lunch with the cool kids. Next, we'll be throwing our cell phones at our assistants."

Rocky gave her best friend a serious look. "No, CeCe," she said. "Promise me, we won't *ever* go all diva."

CeCe thought for a moment. "Not *all* diva," she promised. Then she thought again. "Maybe just a little, *tiny* bit diva." She held up her fingers to show just a small amount. Then she saw Rocky's disapproving stare. "Fine, we're *never* going all diva," she promised.

"Slap swear?" Rocky asked.

CeCe nodded, and the two girls traded face slaps.

"Oh! Ouch!" they both cried.

Rocky shook her head. "Sometimes I miss the pinky swear," she said, rubbing her sore cheek. The bell rang and the two headed off to class. It was time to hit the books and give the diva talk a rest!

CHAPTER 2

ON A QUIET AFTERNOON, Ty and Flynn were hanging out in front of their apartment building. Ty was looking over Flynn's shoulder as he played a video game. But he suddenly stopped paying attention when he saw a pretty girl pass by. He jumped up to the top step. "Hey!" Ty called out, and did a few slick dance moves. He flashed the girl a stellar smile. Then he did the moonwalk and showed her a few more dance moves. "The name is Ty Blue!" he shouted. "Friend me!" he added as the girl smiled and continued walking.

"So wait, girls like guys who dance?" Flynn asked. He had been watching Ty's interaction with the pretty girl very curiously.

"What do you care?" Ty asked as he settled back down on the step.

"Uh, no reason," Flynn said quickly, trying not to give himself away.

Ty saw that look on Flynn's face. He knew it all too well. "Oh, I get it! Little dude's got a crush on a little dudette," he said, chuckling. He put his hand on Flynn's head and rubbed his hair.

"Back off!" Flynn shouted, leaning away from Ty. He tried to smooth down his styled hair. "That takes two hours in the morning," he complained.

"All right, all right," Ty said. "So, does this little

dudette have a name?" He slid down one step to sit closer to Flynn.

A smile spread across Flynn's face. "Destiny," he replied, sighing. Then his eyes lit up.

"Well, do you share your cookies and milk at snack time?" Ty asked, trying not to laugh but failing.

Flynn shot Ty a dirty look. Ty held up his hands innocently. "I'm just kidding," he said. "You like this girl? Well, I'm going to show you a move the ladies will love. Come on." He waved Flynn down the steps to stand next to him on the sidewalk. "Watch me, then you try." Ty did a few quick dance moves. He spun around and pointed to Flynn. "Go," he said.

Flynn looked down at his feet. There was no way he was going to be able to do any of those moves. Ty was an unbelievable dancer! "I'm going to die alone," he mumbled. He knew that his dance moves were certainly not that good!

Ty was optimistic. This situation was going to need some careful attention, but he knew he could do it. For the next few days, he worked with Flynn and tried to teach him to dance.

After about a week, Ty met up again with Flynn outside the apartment building. Ty motioned for him to move down to the sidewalk where there was more room to dance. "All right, kid. Show me what you've got," Ty said. "One, two. One, two, three!"

Flynn did some of the best moves that he had—which wasn't saying all that much, but he had worked hard to mimic some of Ty's dance routines. "Whoo!" he cried as he finished.

"Hey! Good job, little dude," Ty told him.

Just then, a young girl walked by. Ty put his fingers in his mouth and let out a catcall. "Hey!" Ty called.

Flynn watched carefully. "What was that about?" he asked.

"Just getting her attention," Ty said matter-of-factly. He started to head down the steps.

"Oh, no." Flynn held Ty back. "You're not going anywhere till you teach me that."

Ty laughed. "It's easy," he said. "You just put your fingers in your mouth and blow." He demonstrated putting his fingers in his mouth and then blowing. He leaned down to Flynn. "You give it a shot."

Flynn tried and wound up spitting all over Ty!

"All right, little dude, first thing you need to learn," Ty said, wiping his face, "is that if you do *that* again, I'll kill you."

Flynn ran away, but Ty wasn't really mad. In fact, he was pretty confident that he could teach Flynn how to whistle.

A little while later, Flynn was whistling like a champion. Ty sat with Flynn at the bottom of the steps as Flynn catcalled to girls walking by. "Oh, oh, right there," Ty said proudly after Flynn had whistled successfully. He smiled. He had taught the little dude to whistle!

"You're getting good at this," Ty said, eyeing Flynn. He was a great protégé!

Flynn continued to whistle. But a woman who walked past did *not* appreciate the whistle and whacked her large handbag over Ty's head. She had thought the whistling came from him. Ty went flying off the stoop onto the sidewalk!

"Oh," he groaned. He looked up at Flynn. "Yeah, I think you got that down now," Ty said solemnly.

"Okay, can you help me with one last thing?" Flynn had been dying to ask Ty for a while, but he hadn't gotten up the nerve. He slid over to his new buddy. "I try to talk to Destiny, but every time I do, I get scared, freeze up . . ." he said nervously, his voice trailing off.

"Little dude, the key to talking to girls is to listen to them talk," Ty advised. He leaned in closer to his student and smiled coyly. "*Then* pretend to care."

"How do you do that?" Flynn asked. He knew that he had asked the right person for help with this!

"Mostly you nod and say things like 'Uh-huh, I hear you, tell me more, that must have been terrible.'" He put his hand over his heart dramatically.

"So what if I really care about what she's saying and think it's important?" Flynn asked.

"Then you're a girl," Ty told him. He stood up and walked away.

Flynn noted Ty's advice. He was going to be very prepared when he saw Destiny!

CHAPTER 3

AT THE SHAKE IT UP, CHICAGO studio, a rehearsal for the new dance routine was just beginning. The dancers were all watching Eddie, the lead dancer and choreographer. Deuce was there, too. He was busy filming the rehearsal for his documentary.

"Okay, guys, let's take it again from the top," Eddie shouted. "Five, six, seven, eight!"

In the back line of dancers, CeCe leaned over

to Rocky. "This is all we get to do?" she whispered. She frowned. The dance step that she was asked to do was as simple as waving her hands back and forth and stepping side to side. A monkey could have done it! She moved closer to Rocky. "Seriously?" she mumbled.

"Better than dancing alone in the ladies' room!" Rocky exclaimed, keeping a smile on her face. She was just happy to be onstage!

"We had more to do at kindergarten graduation and I was dressed as a zucchini," CeCe complained, remembering her stage debut many years ago.

Gunther Hessenheffer, another background dancer on the show, was standing next to CeCe and couldn't help but eavesdrop. "What's the matter, girlies?" he hissed. "Did you think you were going to be the big stars of the show?" he asked, gesturing to the few lead dancers center stage. They were doing steps far more complicated and seemed to be loving it.

Tinka Hessenheffer, Gunther's sister and also a background dancer, sidled up to her brother. "Gunther and Tinka are willing to doo-doo all day long," she said, raising her arms and executing the dance move they were instructed to do for the number.

"Okay, take five," Eddie suddenly said, turning to the group. Everyone on the dance floor headed to grab some water or rest.

CeCe looked around the studio. She was tired of hanging in the background! "I'll take care of it," she said.

"That's what I'm afraid of," Rocky commented. She watched her friend approach the choreographer.

"Hi, we haven't met yet," CeCe said, turning on her charm full blast. "I'm CeCe, and this is Rocky. We're the new dancers. And *you* are?"

"Eddie," he replied, very distracted. He was

texting on his phone and wasn't at all interested in talking to her.

"And your last name?" CeCe asked, pushing for more information.

Eddie didn't take his eyes off his phone. "Quit bothering me," he said.

"Oh, interesting name!" Rocky replied.

CeCe decided to take charge. "Eddie, there's been a little mistake," she cooed sweetly. She saw him put his phone back in his pocket. Here was her chance to get through to him. She took a deep breath and pleaded her case. "I don't think Gary Wilde would be thrilled that our talent is being wasted in the back." She pointed to the far end of the stage. "Just tell us who we can talk to about this little issue."

"Mmmm," he said. He nodded his head as if he understood where she was coming from. "Well, I'll tell you who you *can't* talk to. *Me!* Or any of the other Wild Things!" He flashed them a forced smile. "We're the lead dancers. You're just the *background* dancers."

Rocky shook her head. "Got it," she said, trying to sound agreeable. Her curiosity got the better of her and she just had to ask one more question. Since the lead dancers had a name, maybe their group did, too! "Do we have a cool nickname?"

"The Rear Ends," Eddie told her.

"I don't suppose you'd think about changing that to ... The Falcons?" Rocky asked dramatically.

"If you don't mind, I'm going to go to my dressing room," Eddie said as kindly as he could manage. He pushed past CeCe and Rocky and walked away.

CeCe's face brightened. "Oh, cool! Do we get dressing rooms?" she asked, following him.

Eddie showed them to an open area with hooks and cubbies. "Right here," he said.

"We get hooks," CeCe said sarcastically. She turned and saw the show's host, Gary Wilde, across the studio. She grabbed Rocky's hand and dragged her over to him. "Gary, we need to talk to you," she said urgently.

Deuce quickly followed behind his friends, video camera in hand. He was getting great footage for his documentary!

Rocky saw Gary's somewhat annoyed expression and tried a different approach. "She means, 'Gary, can we please talk to you'," she said, flashing him a broad smile.

"Of course," he said, smiling back at the girls.

"The Wild Things have this ridiculous idea that we're supposed to stand behind them and be doo-doo girls!" CeCe told him.

Gary raised his eyebrows and put his clipboard down for a second. "*Doo-doo* girls?" he asked, slightly confused.

"You know, doo, doo, doo, doo," CeCe sang out as she swirled her hands in a circle in front of her face.

Gary realized that the girls were thinking they were like old-fashioned doo-wop dancers in a chorus. He nodded now that he understood what they were saying.

CeCe continued, "Oh, and we don't have dressing rooms. We have hooks," she complained.

"Wow," Gary said sympathetically. "Looks like I need to have a little talk with someone."

CeCe breathed a huge sigh of relief. She knew that if she calmly told Gary what was going on, he'd do what he could to fix things! She smiled sweetly at him. "Thank you, Gary." She turned to Rocky. "See, Rocky, if you don't ask for what you want, you don't get it."

Gary shook his head. "Cop a squat," he told the girls.

When Rocky realized that *they* were the people who needed the talk, she moaned. "Uh-oh."

"Oh," CeCe said as she sat down on the spot where she had been standing.

Gary walked around the girls. "Looks like you two starlets are a little short on humility. Yeah, I'll have you know, there was a girl who danced here ten years ago using the same hook as you. And today she's one of the biggest music stars in all of show business."

"Lady Gaga?" Rocky asked, hopefully. The thought of the superstar having been in the same position that they were now in was amazing!

Gary decided to go with that assumption. "Okay," he said. Then he clapped his hands together. "Look, CoCo, Ricky, I like you," he said. "If I didn't, I wouldn't have even bothered to remember your names."

"You didn't," CeCe said. "It's *CeCe*," she said, pointing to herself. "And *Rocky*," she said, pointing to her best friend.

"I don't think so," Gary stated. Then he walked away, but smiled first at Deuce's camera.

"Nice work, CeCe," Rocky said, standing up.

"Just when we thought we were somebodies, we're back to being *nobodies*."

Deuce turned his camera around and spoke into the lens. "They were at the top of the world, then, bang! Doo-doo girls!"

"Look, I think I reacted the way any normal person would have if they were given a hook!" CeCe exclaimed.

Just then, Tinka and Gunther ran up to Gary in their matching gold jackets and black outfits. "Thank you for the hook, Gary," Tinka gushed. "We love it!"

"Look, I crocheted a hook cover," Gunther said, displaying his art project for Gary.

CeCe rolled her eyes. "Like I said, any *normal* person."

While CeCe and Rocky got ready to return to the dance floor, Deuce followed Gary with his camera rolling. Gary was talking to Sid, the producer of the show. Deuce stood back, but focused his camera on the two men.

"We can't afford this many people, Gary. You have to get rid of two," Sid told him. He looked very worried.

"Well, it's not a very difficult decision," Gary replied. "I mean, you know what they say: 'Last hired, first fired'."

Deuce couldn't believe what he had just heard! He scanned the room with his camera and found CeCe and Rocky. He zoomed in on his two friends.

"Just chillax, Rocky," CeCe instructed. She put her hands on Rocky's shoulders. "This'll all blow over by tomorrow."

Deuce took a deep breath. He wondered how he was going to tell Rocky and CeCe the news. He had the makings of a great documentary, but how was he going to tell his friends that they were about to be fired?

CHAPTER 4

LATER THAT EVENING, Deuce was still thinking about what he was going to do. Then he realized that he wouldn't actually have to *tell* them the bad news. He could just show them the camera footage! As he sat in CeCe's living room, he planned how he would ease into it.

"There's something I want you to look at, and you're not going to like it," he told the girls as they walked into the room.

"It's not your infected toe again, is it?" Rocky asked, horrified. She remembered when he had showed her his gross green toenail last week!

"No, but if you want to see that . . ." Deuce began, standing up and taking off his sneaker.

"Oh, come on, Deuce!" Rocky said impatiently. "Sometime today!" She sat down on the couch next to him.

Deuce sat down again. "All right, just don't shoot the messenger," he said. "Also, don't kick him, slap him, or poke him with a sharp stick." He looked right at CeCe to make sure she was on board with the plan. When the girls agreed, Deuce touched a key on his laptop.

The scene between Gary and Sid appeared on the screen. CeCe and Rocky leaned in close to watch. When the girls heard what Gary had told Sid, their mouths fell open in shock!

Deuce closed the laptop. "I'm really sorry, but I thought you should know," he said. He hoped that he had done the right thing by telling his friends.

CeCe blew her bangs off her forehead. This was really bad news!

"I can't believe he's firing us," Rocky said sadly. She put her head in her hands.

"We don't know that," CeCe said.

"'Last hired, first fired'," Rocky repeated.

CeCe nodded her head. "We *were* the last hired," she admitted.

"Well, technically, *you* were the last hired," Rocky told her.

CeCe sighed. This called for a plan. Dancing in the back row on the show was better than not dancing on the show at all!

♪ ♪ ♪

The next day at the *Shake It Up, Chicago* studio, CeCe and Rocky were feeling a bit more optimistic. They had come up with a plan to try and save their jobs. They had brought a box of chocolates to leave in Gary's dressing room, hoping to butter him up.

"I hope Gary likes chocolate," CeCe said hopefully. She saw Gary walking across the studio with the Hessenheffers trailing behind him. The twins were, as usual, in matching glittery outfits.

"Enjoy the vanilla cake, Gary. We know it's your favorite," Gunther told him.

"This is so cool. I've never seen my face on frosting!" Gary told them, admiring the cake. When he spotted CeCe and Rocky, he held it up to show them.

CeCe handed the box of chocolates to Rocky, who turned and dropped them in the garbage can. Clearly, Gunther and Tinka had beaten them to it!

"Thanks, Gustav and Twinkie," Gary gushed happily.

"Actually, I'm Gunther," he said.

"And I'm Tinka," his sister added.

Together, the twins struck a pose and smiled. "And we are the Hessenheffers!"

Gary shook his head. "I don't think so," he said, happier with the names that he had called them. He walked off, leaving the twins speechless.

"Wow," Rocky said, coming up to the brother and sister duo. "I have *never* seen bigger butt-kissers than the two of you."

Their conversation was interrupted when Gary walked by with Sid. "It's ridiculous, Sy," Gary told him. "The cleaning staff has been on strike for two weeks. I mean, you should see my dressing room. It's a pig sty!"

The producer shrugged. "Nothing I can do," he said. "And, by the way, my name isn't *Sy*, it's *Sid*."

"I don't think so," Gary said.

Sid turned around and gave Gary an exasperated look.

Gunther had overheard their conversation

and had an idea. He gave his sister a look, and the two of them took off after Gary. "Oh, Gary!" Gunther called. He held up his hands, begging. "*We* will clean your dressing room! Please, please, please!"

Gary smiled at the twins. "That's why I like you two," he said, grinning. "You're go-getters." He glanced around the studio and then looked down. "And could you do something about this dance floor?" He scrunched up his face as he noticed spots of dirt. "There's *schmutz* everywhere."

"We're go-getters, too!" Rocky said urgently. She rushed over to Gary, with CeCe right behind her. "We'll clean off the *schmutz*!" She paused for a second. "Whatever *schmutz* is," she added nervously.

Gary stared at the two girls. "Great, you do that," he said, patting Rocky on the head.

CeCe sighed. She spun around and checked out the dirty studio dance floor.

"So, are you ready to clean this dirty floor?" Rocky asked her.

Not willing to give up on her dream of staying on the show, CeCe was ready for any challenge. She tried to stay positive. "Show me a sponge, baby, show me a sponge," she said.

Rocky laughed. She knew that CeCe would be willing to do almost anything to stay on *Shake It Up, Chicago*. She just hoped that their plan for staying on the show actually worked!

CHAPTER 5

TY AND FLYNN were once again on the front steps of their apartment building. They were hanging out, practicing some dance moves and watching people walk by.

Just then, Flynn caught sight of a blond girl and stopped in his tracks. His face turned a bright shade of red. "Oh, there's Destiny," he said nervously.

"Whoa, little dude," Ty said, checking out the

beautiful girl. "You left out one tiny detail about Destiny."

"Didn't I mention she's blond?" Flynn asked.

Ty shook his head. "No, you skipped that," he told him. He looked at Destiny again. "Hey, did you notice she's twice your age!" He straightened his jacket and smoothed back his hair. "I'll take it from here," he said, trying to play it cool. He headed down the steps toward her.

Flynn put up his hand. "Back off, stretch," he scolded. He reached out and pulled Ty back to the top step. "I called dibs." He stuck his fingers in his mouth and let out a strong, loud whistle. Ty couldn't help but again be proud of his protégé!

Destiny glanced over her shoulder. She waited until Flynn was at the bottom of the steps. "What do you want, Flynn?" she asked impatiently.

With all the confidence he could muster, Flynn leaned back and tried to act cool. He took a deep breath. "I was wondering if you wanted to come upstairs for a video game," he said. Then he spun around, angled his hands, and pointed at Destiny with a wink. "*And* a fudge pop," he added.

"Not in the mood," Destiny said. Her hair gently swung back and forth against her back. "My cat's sick, my mom's on my case, and the last thing I need is some little kid bugging me." She rolled her eyes and turned to leave.

Flynn moved in closer. "Tell me more," he said, full of sincerity. He winked at Ty. See, he really was listening to all the advice that Ty had given him. Now was his chance to see if Ty's plan to attract the ladies really worked!

Destiny's face softened. "Really?" she asked. "Okay." She walked over to Flynn. "Well, it's mostly my mom. She just has a way of making everything about *her*!"

"I hear you," Flynn said. He stuck his elbow out so that Destiny could grab on to it and he could escort her up to his apartment. "That must be terrible. Go on," he said.

"And don't even get me *started* about my brother," Destiny continued as she headed up the steps with Flynn. "He's been going through all of my stuff," she complained as they walked into the building.

"Man! I'm some kind of freaky genius!" Ty exclaimed as he watched the odd couple stroll inside together. He couldn't help but feel incredibly proud!

A little while later, Flynn and Destiny were sitting on the stoop steps. Destiny was happy to tell Flynn all of her problems. He was such a good listener! Ty peeked out the front door and overheard their conversation.

"And then my dad made me visit my grandmother and it was so boring," Destiny said.

"I hear you. That must be terrible," Flynn said with composure. He couldn't believe how that simple sentence had gotten him so much attention from Destiny!

Ty was not willing to give up the fight for the girl's attention so fast. He squeezed in between Destiny and Flynn on the steps.

"Oh, hey, little dude," he said to Flynn. "*Really little dude*," he said, chuckling. Nothing wrong with pointing out the obvious!

When Flynn and Destiny looked over at him, he seized the opportunity to get Destiny to notice him. "I hope you don't mind," he said very innocently. "I've been in my room playing guitar and writing poetry. Just needed a little exercise."

Destiny gave Ty a sweet look.

Ah, works every time, Ty thought to himself smugly. Mention guitar and poetry, and the girls start to melt.

"Wow, you're really good," Destiny told Ty, following him.

"Uh-huh, I hear you, that must be terrible,"

he commented, giving her a wink.

Destiny laughed.

Not to be outdone, Flynn glared up at Ty. "Watch this!" he called out suddenly. He jumped down the steps to the sidewalk and demonstrated his new dance moves. In his final spin, he faked falling and went down. "Ow, ow, ow, my ankle!" he cried out. He grimaced and rolled on the ground, moaning.

Destiny ran over to Flynn immediately. She helped him up and gave him a hug. "You poor thing!" she gushed. She let him lean on her and helped him walk up the steps.

Peeking over Destiny's shoulder, Flynn caught Ty's eye. "See you later, *sucka*!" he hissed as Destiny helped him upstairs. His date with Destiny would not be interrupted!

Ty shook his head. He definitely had underestimated his student! Flynn was a total ladies' man. He had to admit defeat.

CHAPTER 6

CECE AND ROCKY were not ready to admit defeat either. If the Hessenheffers could clean Gary's dressing room, CeCe and Rocky could clean the dance floor.

"Oh, this is going well," CeCe grunted. They were using toothbrushes and a tube of toothpaste to scrub the floor. It was taking forever! "We should be done by our senior prom."

The Hessenheffers walked by with a bucket

of cleaning supplies and a mop. "Hey, where'd you guys get the cleaning supplies?" CeCe called out.

"Down the hall, turn right, then look for the room we've emptied of all the cleaning supplies," Gunther said, laughing with his sister.

CeCe shrugged. "What are *we* supposed to use?"

Tinka threw a bottle toward her. "Here, pitiful ones. Floor wax. Fetch," she said as she tossed it down. Rocky lunged for the bottle and quickly grabbed it.

"Ever feel like they're winning?" Rocky grunted as the twins walked away, smirking.

CeCe was taking the task very seriously. "Well, now we have floor wax, but we *still* don't have a mop," she said, standing up.

Rocky suddenly had an idea. She gave CeCe a knowing look. "Oh, really?" Rocky asked. She reached over and pulled the hood of CeCe's yellow sweatshirt over her head. "I think I'm looking at one!" Rocky turned CeCe around and squirted floor wax on the back of her sweatshirt. "On your back, Red."

Holding her friend's feet, Rocky swept CeCe around the dance floor, using her as a mop!

"I'm not loving this," CeCe groaned as she was dragged along the floor.

"You loving getting fired more?" Rocky replied.

"No," CeCe admitted. "Mop me, baby."

Rocky twirled CeCe in a circle. "Whoo!" she exclaimed, noticing how clean the floor looked. "The scum is coming right up!"

Rocky moved CeCe to the edge of the dance floor. "I'm starting . . . to think . . . this plan . . . wasn't very well thought out," CeCe grumbled.

Rocky looked around at the shiny, clean dance floor. "Actually, I think the plan is going very well," she said.

"You're enjoying this a little, aren't you?" CeCe asked, noticing Rocky smirking.

Rocky laughed. "No," she replied. "I'm enjoying it a *lot*." She grinned and pulled CeCe around the floor a little faster.

"Whoa!" CeCe shouted. Rocky gave her a bigger push, and CeCe went sliding further across the floor!

"More floor wax," Rocky said. She bent down and squirted more wax over CeCe's sweatshirt.

"Thanks," CeCe said, grimacing. "Chemicals in this cleaner *really* take off the edge of the concussion that you just gave me!" She wrinkled up her nose.

Ignoring her, Rocky continued mopping the floor with her best friend.

"Getting dizzy!" CeCe cried out as Rocky whipped her around.

Just then, the Hessenheffers walked by. Gunther still had on his red cleaning gloves. "We are finished in Gary's dressing room and you can eat off his floor," he announced proudly.

"Which we did," Tinka added. "Gunther brought hummus."

"Mmm, hummus," Gunther said, rubbing his hand on his stomach happily. Then he jumped back as Rocky pushed CeCe toward them. "What are you doing?" he asked.

"I'm using CeCe as a mop," Rocky said matter-of-factly. She put CeCe's feet down and stood with her hands on her hips.

CeCe jumped to her feet. "We waxed this dance floor so it's shiny enough for Gary to see himself in it," she boasted. She faced the twins. "And you know how Gary likes to see himself."

Gunther raised his eyebrows. "Didn't anyone ever tell you don't wax a dance floor?" he asked.

At that moment, Gary ran out of his dressing room and toward the dance floor. "Hey! My dressing room looks . . ." he began to say. He went sliding across the super shiny, waxed floor. "Aah!!!!" he cried as he went crashing into a table. Cups, plates, and food went flying as Gary fell in a heap on the floor.

CeCe and Rocky shared a look of disbelief. They glanced back at Gunther and Tinka. Weren't they the ones who had *given* them the floor wax?

"No," CeCe said slowly, realizing that they had been tricked. "Nobody told us that."

The Hessenheffers grinned. Their sneaky plan had worked!

♪ ♪ ♪

The next morning was Saturday—filming day at *Shake It Up, Chicago*. Rocky climbed through CeCe's apartment window to meet her friend so they could head to the set together.

Rocky threw her bag on the chair. "So, are you ready for our last show ever?" she asked sadly.

"No," CeCe said miserably. They had worked

so hard to get on the show. How could they already be kicked off?

"Me neither," Rocky replied.

"It's all my fault," CeCe said. "I acted like a dumb diva." She took her glass of orange juice and sat down at the kitchen table.

"Hmm," Rocky said thoughtfully. "Hope you're not looking for an argument."

"No. I know I blew it for us," CeCe told her. "I always blow it for us, don't I?"

"Most of the time you're the one who makes things happen," Rocky told her friend, smiling.

"No, I don't," CeCe said, shaking her head.

"Who got us on the show in the first place?" Rocky asked, trying to cheer up CeCe. She stood behind her.

CeCe thought for a moment. "That would be me," she said, laughing.

"And who got us kicked off the show?" Rocky asked.

"That would be me," CeCe slowly admitted.

"See?" Rocky said, walking around CeCe's chair. "You *always* make things happen!"

CeCe felt terrible. She stood up and took Rocky's hand. "I'm really sorry, Rocky," she said.

"It's okay. So, what's your plan?" Rocky asked.

CeCe shifted her feet. "Well, I don't *have* a plan," she confessed.

"Oh, come on, you *always* have a plan," Rocky countered.

CeCe thought for a moment. Then something came to her. "Well, I *do* have an idea," she began.

Rocky smiled. She hoped CeCe's idea could get them back on the show!

CHAPTER 7

ON THE SET, the cameras were cued, and the dancers were in their places. The show was about to begin!

"Here's your host, Gary Wilde!" the announcer bellowed.

The dancers onstage all cheered as Gary ran through the crowd. He gripped the microphone and spoke directly into the camera. "Hello, Chicago!" he exclaimed. He pointed to the people around him. "These are the hottest dancers," he said, then he turned to acknowledge the DJ behind him. "He's spinning the hottest music, and I'm Gary Wilde, and this . . ." Gary took an extra-long dramatic pause. ". . . is *Shake It Up, Chicago*! Whoo!"

Eddie the choreographer counted out the beat, and the lead dancers all started their routine. Their moves were spot on. The background dancers were all doing their routine very well, too.

In the middle of their performance, CeCe turned to Rocky. "Ready?" she asked.

"Let's do this," Rocky said, nodding. She grabbed her friend's hand, and the two girls pushed to the front of the stage.

"Now, Deuce!" CeCe shouted to her friend.

Deuce was backstage, trying to connect a bunch of wires. "The black cable goes to the yellow, the blue goes to the orange," he mumbled to himself. He plugged the last cord in and hoped for the best!

Suddenly, the *Shake It Up, Chicago* logo vanished from the dance floor. In its place appeared a picture of CeCe and Rocky! Their image was on all the monitors and screens. Deuce's plan to showcase the photo of his friends had worked! CeCe and Rocky continued dancing as if nothing had happened. The other dancers had no choice but to form a circle around the girls as CeCe and Rocky stole the show.

Everyone, including Gary and the director, was really confused. At the end of the song, Gary ran onto the stage. "Okay, we'll be right back," he said into the microphone. "Who knows, perhaps we'll have more surprises." He glanced over his shoulder at CeCe and Rocky. "*Or* fewer dancers."

The "Off Air" buzzer sounded, and the cameras and lights dimmed.

Gary walked over to the girls. "You want to

explain *exactly* what you two were doing up here?" he asked.

"Showing you what you're going to miss after you fire us," Rocky said. Their plan was to highlight their best dance moves and prove to Gary that they deserved to be on the show. Rocky thought they had pretty much rocked it.

"No, you're not going to fire us," CeCe went on. "You know why? Because we *quit!*"

Gary looked at the girls quizzically. "Who said anything about firing you?" he asked.

"Who said anything about quitting?" Rocky replied quickly. Maybe they weren't getting fired after all!

"We overheard you saying you were going to fire somebody," CeCe explained.

"Yeah, I am," Gary said. He pointed to two guys who were walking by. "The guy who gets me coffee and the guy who puts cream cheese on my bagel."

"Oh!" CeCe exclaimed, suddenly realizing their huge mistake.

"You will be missed," Gary said to the two guys as they shuffled sadly across the stage.

"In that case, never mind," CeCe said quickly. She put her arm around Rocky. "Forget we ever said anything. Come on, Rocky, let's get to the background where we belong."

Gary gave the girls a stern look. "Step out of line again and you'll be joining the cream-cheese guy," he told them.

"Yes, sir," Rocky promised.

CeCe and Rocky grinned. Their jobs on *Shake It Up, Chicago* were safe after all. They were living their dream as dancers on the best dance show in Chicago . . . and that's where they planned on staying!

THE BEAT GOES ON!

LOOK FOR THE NEXT BOOK
IN DISNEY'S
SHAKE IT UP SERIES!

BRING IT!

Adapted by N.B. Grace

Based on the series created by Chris Thompson

Part One is based on the episode, "Give It Up," written by Rob Lotterstein

Part Two is based on the episode, "Glitz It Up," written by John D. Beck & Ron Hart

CHAPTER 1

THE SET OF *Shake It Up, Chicago* was in full swing, and, as usual, host Gary Wilde was fired up. He stood on the metal riser above the stage, faced the camera, and said into his microphone: "And now, *Shake It Up, Chicago* presents the spotlight dance of the week. Let's hear it for the one, the only, CeCe Jones!"

The lights hit the back of the stage. The audience could see a silhouette of CeCe striking a pose. Then the backdrop parted and she strutted out onto the stage, wearing a shiny gold dress, matching knee-high boots, silver tights, and a gold bow in her long auburn hair. She sparkled under the stage lights as she began to dance.

She wowed the crowd with her fancy moves, and the audience went wild! The soundstage was filled with the sounds of people cheering and applauding–and CeCe loved it!

She smiled as she pulled off a few of her really sophisticated moves. This was the spotlight dance, which meant she was right where she belonged–in the spotlight!

Suddenly, her best friend, Rocky Blue, walked out on the stage with a quizzical look on her face. Unlike CeCe, Rocky was not dressed for a performance. This was unusual because both CeCe and Rocky wanted to be professional dancers. As two of the teen dancers on the

TV dance show *Shake It Up, Chicago*, they were already well on their way to success.

But now, in spite of the fact that the music was pumping and the stage lights were shining, Rocky was wearing a very ordinary outfit—a pink sweater, short plaid skirt, and ankle boots with gray socks. She certainly wasn't dressed for the spotlight dance!

CeCe started to push her friend aside. "Hit the road," she told Rocky. "This is a solo gig."

Rocky sighed. "CeCe, you're asleep. This is a dream," she said.

"I know," CeCe grinned. "A dream come *true!*"

Rocky shook her head, her dark curls cascading around her shoulders. "You don't find it strange that you were making out with Robert Pattinson before you came out here and started dancing?"

CeCe cast her eyes to the ceiling—as if it was odd that she had been kissing the handsome star of the most popular vampire movie ever!

"Don't worry, I didn't let him bite my neck," CeCe replied.

"Okay, if this isn't a dream, then why is Gary Wilde dressed as a giant hot dog, dancing with some mustard?" Rocky asked, pointing offstage.

CeCe looked at where her friend was pointing. Sure enough, the host of the show was dressed in a hot-dog costume. And, he was dancing with someone wearing a costume that looked like a jar of mustard! CeCe's face fell. *Was* this all a dream?

Still asleep in her bed, CeCe pulled her comforter tighter around her. "I'm a star. No, I'm a superstar. I'm a star," she said, muttering to herself.

"Wake up," Rocky said softly, giving her a gentle nudge.

CeCe slept on.

Rocky tried again. "Wake up," she murmured.

CeCe snuggled deeper into her bed.

"Wake up!" Rocky yelled.

"Aah!" CeCe jerked awake. "Oh, hey, Rocky. I was having a dream and you were there, and Gary Wilde was a hot dog dancing with some mustard. What do you think that's about?"

Rocky chuckled and rolled her eyes. "Um, that you shouldn't have eaten four hot dogs last night."

"Wow," CeCe said, impressed. "You're good."

Rocky brushed off CeCe's last comment. It was time to get down to business. "Okay, get up, get dressed. You know Mrs. Locassio from the third floor?"

"The woman who doesn't like you?"

Rocky frowned. "She *does* like me," she insisted. "*Everyone* likes me! Anyway, I volunteered us at her senior center, and we're going to perform for them this morning."

This news made CeCe clutch her pillow tightly. "Senior center? Unless you're talking about high school seniors, I'm going back to sleep."

But Rocky was adamant. "Wake up," she insisted, grabbing a pillow and hitting CeCe with it.

"I'm up, I'm up, I'm up!" CeCe exclaimed. It looked like her best friend simply wasn't going to take no for an answer! Like it or not, she had some volunteering to do!